MOMOTARŌ AND THE ISLAND OF OGRES

Momotarō AND THE Island of Ogres

A Japanese folktale as told by

STEPHANIE WADA

Paintings by

KANO NAGANOBU

GEORGE BRAZILLER / NEW YORK

First published in the United States of America by George Braziller, Inc., in 2005

The paintings are reproduced from a pair of handscrolls in the Spencer Collection of
The New York Public Library entitled *Momotarō Emaki* (The Scroll of the Tale of the Peach Boy)
painted by Isen'in, Kano Naganobu. Early nineteenth century, Japan; ink, color, and gold on silk;
scroll 1: 31.9 x 893.7 cm, scroll 2: 31.9 x 933 cm; Spencer Coll. Japanese MS 202.

For information, please address the publisher:
George Braziller, Inc.
171 Madison Avenue
New York, NY 10016
www.georgebraziller.com

Library of Congress Cataloging-in-Publication Data:
Wada, Stephanie.
Momotarō and the island of ogres : a Japanese folktale / as told by
Stephanie Wada ; illustrations by Kano Naganobu.—1st ed.
p. cm.
Summary: Found floating on the river inside a peach by an old couple, Momotarō
grows up and fights the terrible demons who have terrorized the village for years.
ISBN 0-8076-1552-8 (hardcover)
[1. Folklore—Japan.] I. Naganobu, Kano, 1775–1828, ill. II. Title.
PZ8.1.W113Mo 2005
398.2'0952'01—dc22   2004027570

Case stamping: In black, the artist's signature (Isen'in in Hōin Fujiwara
Naganobu hitsu), and in red, his seal (Genshōsai)

Designed by Rita Lascaro

Printed and bound in Singapore

First edition

Momotarō-san, Momotarō-san

Okoshi ni tsuketa kibi-dango

Hitotsu watashi ni kudasai na.

Agemashō, agemashō

Kore kara oni no seibatsu ni

Tsuite yuku nara agemashō!

Momotarō-san, Momotarō-san

Please give me one of those

Millet dumplings you're carrying.

I'd gladly give one to you,

If you'll go along with me

To conquer the ogres!

Japanese folk song

Deep in the countryside of Japan, a long, long time ago, there lived an elderly woodcutter and his wife. They were very lonely, for their cottage was a great distance away from any towns or villages, and in spite of all their prayers, they had no children. Almost every day the old man went into the mountains to cut wood, which he sold to farmers in the valley, while his wife busied herself with household chores and tended to their small vegetable garden.

Early one spring morning, when the mist hung low over the ground and drops of dew hung from the tip of every leaf and reed, the woodcutter headed for the mountain forest and his wife set off for the river with a bundle of laundry. Imagine her astonishment when she saw what looked like a great, gilded orb bouncing and bobbing in the eddies of the current. As the water brought it closer to the bank, she saw that it was an enormous peach, glowing pink and golden in the light of the rising sun. Quickly, she snatched it up and took it back to the cottage, thinking how pleased her husband would be to enjoy such an unexpected treat with their daily meal.

By the time the woodcutter returned home for lunch, the morning mist had almost burned away, and sunbeams glinted on the pink and white flowers just coming into bloom on the tree beside the little, thatch-roofed house. As they were far too poor to eat rice very often, the old woman set out a humble meal of millet gruel. Then she proudly displayed the wonderful peach. "Good heavens!" cried the woodcutter. "How delicious it looks. Let's eat it immediately!" His wife began to cut the peach in half and then cried out in amazement, for nestled in the center, where the pit should have been, was a tiny but beautiful baby boy.

"This is surely a gift from the gods," they exclaimed, after the wife told her husband how the peach had come to her. "We will be lonely no longer. This child is an answer to our prayers." Then and there they decided to raise the infant as their son and named him Momotarō, or Peach Boy, in honor of his miraculous arrival.

With the loving care of his adoptive parents, Momotarō soon grew tall and strong. He was by far the handsomest boy in all the countryside and so good-hearted that everyone loved him. His daring and boldness was such that he could face down any of the dangerous creatures of the woodland, but because of his kind nature, the wild animals he defeated quickly became his friends. He wandered the misty mountains and deep ravines near his home without a trace of fear in his heart. Once, in the mountain forest, the fiercest of all beasts—a great bear—charged toward him with a roar. Momotarō caught the bear in a wrestler's grip and flung him to the earth.

By the time Momotarō was fifteen years old not even grown men could match him for strength and bravery. He also had wisdom far beyond his age. He and the old couple were very happy together, for he had grown to be a fine young man. Even now, after so many years, the woodcutter and his wife never stopped wondering how it was that such good fortune had come to them.

One day, Momotarō came to the old couple and said, "Mother, Father, I am so grateful for the love and care you have given me. No one could ask for better parents, and I thank you from the bottom of my heart."

The pair looked at him in surprise. "But of course we did our best for you. It was our duty," the woodcutter's wife replied. "And we love you more than words can say. As for thanking us, there is no need to do that. For someday you will look after our welfare, just as we looked after you when you were a small child. That is the way things should be, after all."

Momotarō gave them a serious look. "Well," he said, "that is what I wish to do, but first you must let me go away for a little while. There is something I need to do that will bring good to other people and also bring good to you. A long way away from here there is an island in the sea, Onigashima, the Island of Ogres. I have heard that its inhabitants often ravage the mainland, stealing goods from the rich and poor alike and killing all who try to stop them. These wicked creatures flout the laws of our kingdom and of the gods. I plan to vanquish these demons and return the treasure they have stolen to its rightful owners!"

Although Momotarō was still only a boy of fifteen, the couple decided to let him go. They knew he was stronger and braver than any man alive, and since he had been sent to them by the gods, they felt that only he could defeat the terrible ogres of Onigashima. While Momotarō prepared to leave, the old woman made some delicious millet dumplings called *kibi-dango*, her son's favorite food, so that he could take them on his journey.

After bidding his parents a fond farewell and promising to return as soon as he completed his mission, Momotarō took his parcel of dumplings and headed off in the direction of the northeastern coast. It was a warm, pleasant day, and irises were blooming along the bank of the river. He walked along confidently, following the road, and when midday arrived he sat down on a rock, pulled out his *kibi-dango*, and began to eat.

Suddenly, a large spotted dog ran up to him. "How dare you pass through my meadow without asking my permission. Go back, or I shall bite you to death!"

Momotarō did not move. "Do you know who I am, dog?" he asked. "I am Momotarō, and I am on my way to Onigashima to conquer the ogres and win back their stolen treasure. If you try to stop me, it is you who will be sorry!"

The dog bowed down to the ground. "Forgive me, Momotarō!" he howled with his tail between his legs. "I have heard of your great strength from the other animals. Let me come with you, and I will do whatever I can to help you in your quest."

"Very well," said Momotarō, and he gave the dog a millet dumpling as a reward.

The two walked along the road, and by and by they encountered a monkey. The dog and monkey flew at each other and began to fight, but Momotarō hastily put a stop to their quarreling.

"We are traveling to Onigashima to vanquish the ogres," he explained to the monkey. "If you join us, I'll give you one of these *kibi-dango* to eat!"

The monkey agreed, and the three continued on their way. The dog and the monkey still eyed each another angrily, though, so Momotarō had one walk ahead of him and the other behind.

Farther along the way, a beautiful bird with gleaming plumage and a splendid long tail swooped down in front of them. At once the dog tried to grab it by the neck, as dogs will do with birds, but the pheasant—for that is what it was—defended itself mightily with its sharp claws and beak.

Momotarō pulled them apart and shouted, "Stop fighting, you two! Pheasant, I see that you are a courageous fighter. The dog, the monkey, and I are on our way to defeat the ogres of Onigashima. If you care to join us, I will give you a *kibi-dango* to eat."

The pheasant was happy to be part of the group, and the foursome marched on toward the coast. However, the three animals snarled at each other as they went and bickered constantly.

Finally, Momotarō stopped and spoke sternly to them: "Now look here, you three! How can we be an army if we cannot get along with each other? For the sake of the common good you must put aside your differences and work together as a team. Otherwise, it will be impossible to defeat the ogres. If you disagree, I will go on by myself!"

The animals were ashamed and begged Momotarō's pardon.

In harmony at last, Momotarō and his band marched on across lovely meadows and valleys filled with flowering plants and crisscrossed by fast-running streams. Before they reached the sea they would have to find their way through a stony mountain range that stood before them like a wall, its peaks wreathed in mist and clouds. The four followed a narrow path into the mountains, where moss hung dripping above their heads and the wind blew damp and cold all around them. In spite of his friends' promises, Momotarō worried that they might fall to squabbling again, so he sent one ahead to walk in front, carrying his standard, while the others walked behind him in single file, bearing his weapons.

After many days of traveling along winding paths above narrow gorges and through high mountain passes, it seemed as though they would never reach the coast. Finally, as autumn colors began to make their first appearance, they saw a break in the mountains ahead and smelled the salty air of the sea.

The next evening, with the moon looming above them in the sky, the little band descended from the mountains and caught their first glimpse of the sea in the distance.

None of them had ever seen the sea before. The three animals, brave as they had been during their long and tiring journey, trembled at the sight of the vast expanse of water stretching to the horizon. Only Momotarō did not waver. His bold nature rejoiced that they had come so close to their goal. If only they could see the ogres' island! But they could see nothing but water and the mountains on the other side of the bay.

"Let us go farther along the shoreline," Momotarō suggested. "Perhaps we can see Onigashima when we get past the bay."

His companions sighed at the thought of taking even another step, but they had come so far that it would have been foolish to turn back. And so they continued along the cliffs above the beach until they came to the very end of the bay.

There was a bluff overlooking the water, and as they stood there they could see, in the distance, a forbidding island of stony, dark crags filled with shadow. Gray clouds hung above its jagged peaks.

"Aha!" said Momotarō, pointing. "That must be Onigashima. Let us go down to the beach and find a boat to take us across."

When they reached the seashore, they found, naturally enough, that not a single boatman was willing to make the crossing to the Island of Ogres. Finally, Momotarō was able to obtain a small boat for himself and his crew. They hoisted their few belongings onboard and set Momotarō's standard upright on the prow. When all was ready, they shoved off and headed out to sea, with the dog at the tiller and the monkey manning the oars. The wind was brisk but warm, and the weather quite pleasant, so before long they were all in quite good humor as the boat skimmed over the surface of the water and the sunlight turned the wavelets around them gold.

As they sped over the water the foursome entertained each other with stories of their other adventures. Before long the sinister peaks of Onigashima appeared on the horizon.

"Momotarō!" shouted the pheasant. "Shall I fly ahead to see what awaits us?"

"By all means," agreed Momotarō, and the pheasant spread his wings and flew toward the rocky beach of the Island of Ogres. When he got closer he could see a wall of stone beyond the beach and a mighty wooden gate reinforced with

iron. Several ogres were standing guard before it. They were fearsome brutes—some blue, some red, and some green.

The pheasant glided down until he was right above them. "Run for your lives, or surrender immediately!" he cried. "The great general Momotarō is here to lay siege to your castle and take back the treasure you stole from the mainland."

The ogres all roared with laughter, shaking their horned heads and rolling their eyes. But, for prudence's sake, they retreated behind the massive gate and barred it shut.

When Momotarō landed his little boat, he found not a single ogre on the beach. However, the dog's keen ears could hear an army of them howling with rage and beating their weapons against the ground behind the fortress gate. Quickly the monkey scrambled up the boulders next to the gate, while the pheasant perched on top of the giant crossbeam. Momotarō tried the gates but of course found them firmly shut.

"This is only delaying the battle!" he called to the ogres within. A moment later, he and the dog rushed the gates—the dog with a great mallet and Momotarō with the strength of his muscular arms. Before the ogres realized what was happening, the heavy gates gave way and fell down, and Momotarō, the pheasant, the monkey, and the dog were inside.

The ogres were astounded but not particularly fearful. After all, there were only four invaders, and they themselves were many in number. They raced toward Momotarō, yelling ferociously and brandishing their spears.

28

What a battle it was! Once within the stony abode of the ogres, the little band found itself facing a horde of monsters whose shrieks echoed off the walls of rock all around them. The pheasant flew from ogre to ogre, pecking at their eyes and the tops of their heads and beating their ears with his powerful wings. The monkey and the dog flung themselves into the mass of ogres, biting and scratching, knocking them down and seizing their weapons. The largest ogres tried to kill Momotarō with their spears, but he parried their blows, first with his war fan, which he held closed in his hand, and then with his sword. The creatures began to waver and hesitate as Momotarō's band pressed forward. Before long the ogres were fleeing back into the mountain fastness of the island. There was nowhere to escape, however, for the pheasant flew after them, while Momotarō and the others pursued them swiftly on foot.

In a very brief time the ogres realized that they would have to surrender—or lose their own lives.

The frightened ogres threw down their arms and surrendered.

"You must all promise to stop raiding and pillaging the mainland," Momotarō pronounced. "And you must give back all that you stole from the people there. Furthermore, you must turn over your weapons and swear an oath of allegiance to me, to guarantee your good behavior. Finally, your king must take an oath in my presence—and yours—to live peacefully forever more."

The ogres grimaced and tugged at their horns in frustration but realized that they had no choice. They swore to bring out all of the treasure from their secret caves and called to their companions to come out of hiding. Slowly, the rest of the ogre army crept out from behind the rocks, where they had been crouching in terror. Then the women, children, and elderly ogres emerged from the deep mountain caves, where they had hidden themselves during the battle.

The last to emerge from the caves was the ogre king. He knelt before Momotarō and his companions in his royal robes, with his *shaku*, or scepter of authority, in his hands, and took an oath that he and his people would give up their demonic ways.

"I cannot hold my fortress against you, Lord Momotarō," he said, lowering his forehead to the ground. "I own that we are vanquished. Please spare our lives, and we will make amends for our behavior."

"How can you do that?" the dog snarled. "Ogres only know how to do evil."

"We can learn," the ogre king replied humbly. "We are tough and strong and do not fear hard work or bad weather. If you allow it, we will become fishermen, for we have traveled so often to the mainland that we have become skilled sailors."

"Just see to it that you never trouble the mainland again," Momotarō said severely, and the ogre king swore that they would not.

"If you turn over a new leaf and follow the laws of gods and men, we will leave your island in peace," Momotarō proclaimed. "And as for the stolen treasure, my companions and I will see to it that it is returned."

The dog, the monkey, and the pheasant looked doubtful, but after the king handed his scepter to Momotarō and ordered his men to fetch the treasure from the caves, they realized that the ogres had been won over by Momotarō's generosity as well as by his strength.

The ogre king invited Momotarō and his friends into his rocky grotto for a feast to celebrate their pact.

He clapped his hands, and attendants came rushing to wait upon his guests. A splendid meal, complete with all sorts of delicacies, was set before them on lacquer trays, in stacked lacquer picnic boxes, and on elegantly glazed ceramic plates. Wine was poured from a golden ewer. Ogre musicians played instruments and sang, while others danced for their entertainment. Ogre servants saw to it that Momotarō was comfortably seated and massaged his shoulders. Other servants brought him delicious tidbits from the food and sweets heaped upon the many plates and trays. The dog, monkey, and pheasant each ate their fill, clapped their hands to the music, and enjoyed the dancing. As they ate and drank, the king told Momotarō tales of his ogre clan and of their island kingdom. In this way they enjoyed themselves for the rest of the afternoon.

When the festivities came to an end, Momotarō thanked the king and said that he must be going.

"We will have the treasure brought to you at once!" said the ogre king.

The king and Momotarō rose from their seats in the stony hall, and more servants came in to sweep and tidy up the remains of the banquet. The king led Momotarō's band to a clearing among the mountains and boulders and sent his followers to fetch the stolen riches from his secret caves. All of the other demons gathered around to watch. There was a rumbling sound from within the mountains, and suddenly the demon soldiers told them all to make way. The crowd parted as a massive oxcart, heavily laden with precious goods, emerged from the mouth of the largest cave. Momotarō and his friends had never even imagined such wealth.

"You may take one of our ships for your return to the mainland, Lord Momotarō!" the ogres cried, bowing low.

"Please take the treasure down to the ship and load it for my return journey," Momotarō replied. He and his companions said their farewells to the ogre court, adding a few final stern injunctions to stand by their oath and abandon their thieving ways.

A procession of ogres, led by a group of colorfully clad musicians playing horns, flutes, cymbals, and stringed instruments, slowly made its way toward the beach. Behind them came the heavy cart, pulled by a handsome black ox. The riches it carried were quite a sight: gold, silver, mother-of-pearl, and precious gems, boxes of powdered metal, bolts of fine silk, branches of coral from the sea, furs, embroidered cloths, rare incense, and many other things. Strange as it may seem, the ogres seemed almost happy to be giving up their ill-gotten wealth, for they sang and danced all the way to the shore, waving their arms and shaking their shaggy heads with glee.

Along the route other ogres peered out of their caves to watch the fantastic caravan go by.

At the end of the procession came Momotarō, riding in a magnificent open palanquin. It was so beautifully lacquered and gilded that it gleamed in the early evening light. His intrepid companions walked alongside, carrying his standard and his weapons. Ogres attended them, bearing gifts from the king and the remainder of their belongings. How handsome and regal Momotarō looked—like a true prince of men! The dog, monkey, pheasant, and even the ogres thought, "Surely this boy was sent to earth by the gods to help banish evil from the land."

When they reached the beach, Momotarō found that his little boat had been replaced by a much larger craft—a luxurious ship with a tall mast, just the right size to hold all of the treasure. With the aid of the ogres, the band loaded everything on board and prepared to set sail for the mainland.

With a young ogre at the tiller, the ship seemed to fly over the waves as they sailed away from Onigashima. The deep gold of the evening light shone on the water, on the clouds, and on the mighty cone of Mount Fuji in the distance. The four travelers were filled with excitement at the thought of returning home.

Once on shore, Momotarō's band spent the next few weeks returning the precious objects to their rightful owners. There was treasure enough left over for Momotarō and his parents to live in great comfort for the rest of their lives. The

dog, monkey, and pheasant had no desire for riches. They were pleased merely to accompany Momotarō back to his parents' mountain, where they planned to remain with him as his helpers and comrades-in-arms.

As amazed as Momotarō's parents were with the wealth that he brought, it was the sight of their son at home once again that gave them the most profound joy. Momotarō settled them into a fine house, and they and their animal friends lived there in harmony for many, many years.

POSTSCRIPT

About the Scrolls

These extraordinary paintings of Momotarō's story were created by a Japanese artist named Kano Naganobu, who lived from 1775 to 1828. Painted in ink, colors, and gold on silk, the original images do not exist as separate paintings or scenes, but as a pair of handscrolls. The first scroll follows Momotarō's story until he and his animal friends are about to arrive at Onigashima. The second scroll illustrates the battle between Momotarō's band and the fearsome ogres, the surrender of the ogre king, and the return home. At the end of each scroll are the artist's signature and his rectangular seal stamped in crimson ink.

A handscroll is always kept rolled up when not in use. When viewed, it is unrolled from right to left and the pictures are enjoyed in the same way, starting at the right and moving toward the left. This is customary in Japan as well as in China and Korea, where writing moves from right to left. In the Western world, books are read in the opposite direction (that is, from left to right). If a scroll's illustrations are continuous, with no breaks between them, as in the Momotarō handscrolls, the experience is similar to that of watching a film, with the scenes unfolding one after another.

A closer look at Kano Naganobu's illustrations reveals a number of symbols of long life and good luck that the Japanese had used for centuries in art and literature. Water, which brought the magical peach to Momotarō's mother, was seen as the abode of many spirits. Water and clouds were also seen as the home of the dragon, a popular emblem of good fortune, unlike the fire-breathing, evil dragons of European fairy tales. The peach itself was associated with long life and even immortality. In ancient China, peaches that gave eternal life to whomever ate them were believed to grow in a mountain paradise tended by the mythical Queen Mother of the West. The Japanese were familiar with this Chinese legend and occasionally used peach designs in works of art.

Yet another symbol of immortality throughout East Asia was the crane. In the very first illustration from the scrolls, cranes are shown in flight above the stream where the woodcutter's wife finds the peach (see p. 6). Another scene, in which the ogres hold a feast for Momotarō, shows standing behind the ogre king a screen painted with a crane family of two adult birds and a chick (see p. 34). Finally, what is today one of the most famous symbols of Japan appears in the last scene: the majestic cone of Mount Fuji rising above mist-shrouded hills (see pp. 42–43). A beloved subject for Japanese poets and painters, Mount Fuji had been viewed as a sacred peak since ancient times. The mountain was visible from the city of Edo (now called Tokyo), and to someone living there, like the artist Naganobu, it was an everyday reminder of the power of nature and of the gods who watched over the country from their own special realm.

Like many artists of his day, who often used more than one name, depending on their age, official position, or title, Naganobu was also known as Eishin and, in the later years of his life, as Isen'in. (In Japan, as in China, the family name is given first and the personal name last, the equivalent of "Smith John" or "Van Gogh Vincent.") The school, or studio, of painting to which Naganobu belonged, the Kano School, was one of the most important groups of artists of the time. Although other schools of painting existed in cities like Kyoto and Edo, wealthy lords, government officials, and even temple priests often went to Kano artists. These artists made paintings in ink on paper, paintings in brilliant colors on folding screens covered with gold leaf, paintings on sliding door-panels, hanging scrolls, handscrolls, and fans. Wealthy customers told the artists what kind of picture they wanted, and the artists did their best to oblige.

Naganobu's father, Kano Korenobu, also belonged to the Kano School. It is very likely that Korenobu taught his son to paint in the styles practiced by all Kano artists and that, like other artists, Naganobu also learned painting techniques by copying old masterpieces. He eventually succeeded his father as head of one of the school's branch studios in Edo, where he became official painter to Japan's military government, the Tokugawa shogunate.* Favored artists of the Kano

---

* During the time that Naganobu painted the Momotarō scrolls, Japan actually had two "rulers." One was the emperor, who worked with his court to preserve Japan's ancient traditions of art and culture. He, however, was ruler in name only. It was the other ruler, the shogun, who actually ran the government with the help of samurai administrators and other officials.

School worked as painters to military rulers throughout the Edo period (1615–1868), and for Naganobu to be named one of these official painters was a great honor. It also meant that many other people would want to purchase paintings by him.

We do not know for whom Naganobu made this imaginative, wonderfully painted set of Momotarō handscrolls. As the work was painted on silk, rather than on paper, using gold and finely ground mineral paints of excellent quality, it was obviously made for a well-to-do family or individual—perhaps for a youthful member of a high-ranking samurai clan or for someone destined to be a government official defending the law. There is no doubt that the handscrolls would have made a beautiful gift for either recipient.

About the Story

The story of Momotarō's adventures was very popular before Naganobu painted these handscrolls; at least one earlier illustrated version of the story exists. The tale remained one of the best-loved folk stories of the Edo period and was even turned into stage plays for the theater. The story was so well-known, in fact, that the woodblock-print artist Suzuki Harunobu (1725–1770) created a playful picture as a type of joke, showing a beautiful girl, rather than a baby boy, inside a newly opened peach.

The immense popularity of Momotarō's tale—at least among adults—was partly due to its message: cooperate with members of the group, obey the laws of the ruler, defend the land against wicked lawbreakers, honor one's parents, and look after them when they are old. Children, on the other hand, enjoyed the story as an exciting tale about a boy who almost single-handedly defeats a group of treasure-raiding strangers from across the sea. Perhaps the ogres of Onigashima were inspired by the real pirates who plagued the coast of Japan from time to time. It is possible, too, that the original Momotarō story was composed in the late 1500s or early 1600s, about the time that European ships first arrived in Japan, bringing Portuguese, and later, Spanish, English, and Dutch sailors and traders to the land. The strange clothes, weapons, and jewelry brought by these very different-looking foreigners from the other side of the world seemed like rare and wonderful treasures to the Japanese. The idea of making a story about great riches from a faraway island may have been inspired by these European visitors.

Just as there are different versions of fairy tales like Snow White and the Sleeping Beauty, many Japanese stories and legends exist in different forms. This is true of the account of Momotarō's adventures. There are several details that vary in the written versions of the story, and there are some versions that suggest that storytellers sometimes added events taken from other, older stories. One example of this kind of borrowing is the third scene in Nabanobu's scrolls, which shows a young Momotarō winning a wrestling match with a bear (see p. 10). As there is no bear-wrestling episode in the basic Momotarō story, someone who has read the story elsewhere might ask why the artist created this picture. In Japan, however, lovers of folklore might recognize it as an episode borrowed from the escapades of another legendary boy of great strength, the mighty Kintarō. According to legend, the rambunctious, forest-dwelling Kintarō, whose name means Golden Boy, was so strong that he defeated a bear in a wrestling contest even before he grew to manhood. Later woodblock-print pictures of Kintarō sometimes show him lifting the bear above his head in a wrestling grip or even riding on its back. Why did the artist Naganobu include this scene in his Momotarō illustrations? Perhaps because of the similarities between the Momotarō and Kintarō characters. Or perhaps because the bear-wrestling episode adds action and excitement to the first part of the story, long before the viewer meets the ogres of Onigashima.

Today, images of Momotarō and his animal companions can be found where you might least expect them—next to a sacred shrine, for example, or as a statue in front of a modern-day train station. One region called Okayama Prefecture in western Japan boasts an especially close connection with Momotarō the folk hero: it is famous for its peaches and for its *kibi-dango* (millet dumplings), and one of its old legends tells of a prince who defeated a terrifying ogre on the region's Kibi Plain. Perhaps stories of this mythical prince also contributed to the creation of the Momotarō folktale. Speculation is tempting, but the story's exact origins may forever remain scattered among bits and pieces of the other historical accounts and folktales memorized and handed down by generations of townspeople and country people, of aristocrats and commoners of old Japan.